Helen Orme taught for many years before giving up teaching to write full-time. At the last count she had written over 70 books.

She writes both fiction and non-fiction, but at present is concentrating on fiction for older readers.

Helen also runs writing workshops for children and courses for teachers in both primary and secondary schools.

Kitchen Chaos

by

Helen Orme

Kitchen Chaos
by Helen Orme
Illustrated by Chris Askham

Published by Ransom Publishing Ltd.
Unit 7, Brocklands Farm, West Meon, Hampshire GU32 1JN, UK
www.ransom.co.uk

ISBN   978 184167 152 9
First published in 2013
Reprinted 2014, 2015, 2016 (twice)
Copyright © 2013 Ransom Publishing Ltd.

Illustrations copyright © 2013 Chris Askham

A CIP catalogue record of this book is available from the British Library.

Siti Musa

Wall · Photos · Friends

Hi! I'm Siti Musa.

Siti is a Swahili (African) name meaning 'Lady'.

I'm the oldest in my family. I have two brothers, Daudi and Hanif, and a kid sister Afia.

My dad is a deputy head at our school, which can be bad news sometimes!

My mum is a social worker.

Lu Clarke

Wall · Photos · Friends

I'm Lu Clarke and I'm an only child. My dad is a businessman – he has an IT office in the town centre. My mum, who is Chinese, works in a bank.

My mum's parents (Po-po and Gong-gong – our name for grandparents) live by the sea. They used to have a Chinese restaurant and my mum worked there when she was younger. My other grandparents live close to us.

My parents want the best for me – but they don't always ask me what *I* want.

Kelly Jonson

Wall Photos Friends

I'm Kelly Jonson.

My mum is a single parent. She works as a solicitor. I've got an older brother, Jamie. His girlfriend is Susie.

My parents split when I was very young, and Dad remarried. We don't have any contact with Dad and his new family.

I really want to be a writer – oh, and I fancy Gary! I've decided that I want to be a vegetarian.

Rachel Phillips

Wall · Photos · Friends

I'm Rachel Phillips.

My parents split about 4 years ago. Dad runs a small printing business, and Mum is office manager at our school.

I live with Mum and spend weekends with Dad. His new wife is Janine. They have two young children, a boy and a new baby girl. It's O.K. visiting them, but I'd rather be with Mum.

My older brother Wil is at sixth-form college.

Donna Mills

Wall · Photos · Friends

I'm Donna Mills.

My dad's a bus driver and my mum works in a shop.

I have two older sisters, Marie and Briony. Marie's friend Susie is Kelly's brother's girlfriend.

My brother, Michael, is the youngest.

I love animals and going swimming. There isn't much spare cash in our family – which makes things hard sometimes.

Chapter

1

'I wish it was summer,' moaned Lu. 'It's too cold to have a day off school.'

'What are we going to do?' asked Kelly.

'I don't want to stay at home,' said Siti. 'Dad's got to go into school and Mum will make me look after the little ones if she thinks I've got nothing to do.'

Their school was to be closed the next day and they were planning what to do.

'We could go to the shopping centre,' suggested Lu.

'I haven't got any money,' said Donna.

'What about the museum?' asked Siti. 'That's free.'

'Yeah, but it's boring,' said Lu.

'True,' added Kelly. 'They've only got four rooms.'

'The Library then? It's warm there.' Siti was still trying.

'Boring!' That was Lu again.

'Well you think of something!' Siti was starting to get cross.

'I've got an idea,' said Rachel.

'I hope it's better than Siti's,' said Lu. She was getting cross too.

'I think so,' said Rachel. 'It's my mum's birthday tomorrow, and she's got to go to work too. The school office still needs people, even though we've got the day off.'

'So what?' snapped Lu.

'Oh give her a chance,' said Siti.

'Stop it you two,' said Kelly. 'Go on, Rachel.'

Chapter

2

'I thought we could cook her something nice for tea.'

'That would be fun,' said Lu. She liked cooking.

'We could make her a cake, too,' said Donna.

'And decorate it,' said Kelly.

'We'll have the whole day to do it,' said Rachel.

* * * * *

Next morning, they met at Rachel's house quite early.

Lu had brought some eggs and sugar. 'My mum gave me a recipe for the cake. She said we've got to cook that first if we want to put icing and stuff on it.'

'We'll make it a real party,' said Siti.

'What else can we make?' asked Donna.

'What's your mum got in the cupboard, Rachel?' asked Lu. 'That might give us some ideas.'

Rachel took out a tin of sardines. 'We could make some sandwiches. Mum likes sardines.'

'What about sausage rolls? You need sausage rolls for a party.'

'I think there's some sausages in the freezer.'

Kelly started getting out things they might need.

'Here's more eggs, and flour.'

Lu took them. 'Have you got anything else, Rachel?'

'There's some burgers. But Mum wouldn't like those much.'

Chapter
3

'No, but we could have them for lunch,' said Donna. 'All this talk about food is making me hungry.'

'What about me?' moaned Kelly. 'I'm not going to eat dead animal meat.'

'You can have bread and cheese,' said Lu.

Things were getting busy. Rachel was pulling things out of cupboards and stacking them on the table. It was beginning to get to be a bit of a problem. Every flat space was filling up fast. And Rachel's kitchen wasn't very big.

She got out a big tin of syrup and put it on the edge of the table, next to the flour.

'Look out! It's going to fall,' called Donna. She pushed Rachel to one side and grabbed for the tin.

Donna caught the tin but hit the flour, which fell to the floor. The bag was open and, when it landed, a cloud of flour flew up. All over the floor!

And the table!

And the cat's food dish!

And on the cat, which rushed out of the kitchen and into the hall.

'What are we going to do? My mum will kill me!'

Siti took charge.

'We've got to get organised,' she said. And she started to tell people what to do. For once, even Lu didn't argue.

Chapter

4

Siti got a dustpan to sweep up the flour. By the time she'd finished she was covered too. She went up to the bathroom to get it off.

Lu started mixing things. Rachel found the cake tin, and the other three tidied up and started washing up.

By the time they had finished, the cake was cooked. Rachel took it out of the oven.

'Great!' said Lu. 'It looks perfect.'

'Lunch time!' said Rachel and went to the freezer to get the burgers. 'Oh no!'

'What's the matter?' asked Kelly.

'I forgot to get the sausages out. You have to defrost them before you cook them.'

'It doesn't matter,' said Donna. 'We can use the microwave.'

They took their food into the living room. But there was a nasty surprise there.

Siti had left floury footprints all through the hall and up the stairs. So had the cat! Except the cat's footprints were all over the furniture too!

'Clean-up time, again,' said Donna.

They were busy cleaning when they heard the back door open and close.

'Hi!' It was Wil, Rachel's brother.

Then Wil walked in. He was eating a very big slice of cake!

Chapter
5

They rushed into the kitchen. That slice wasn't even his first. A huge chunk was missing.

'What are we going to do?' wailed Rachel.

'We can cut it into slices,' said Siti.

'We'd better get on with the rest,' said Kelly. 'I'll make the sardine sandwiches.'

Donna got the sausages and put them in the microwave. Siti started work on the cake.

But, somehow, nothing went right.

The cake crumbled as Siti cut it. It tasted good but looked awful!

The sardines were in tomato sauce, and after a few minutes the sandwiches looked like Halloween food!

And Donna forgot to use 'defrost' on the microwave. The sausages came out like lumps of wood.

Rachel sat down and started to cry.

'I've got an idea,' said Siti. 'We'll clear
everything up and order a pizza.'

'I've got a better idea,' said Lu.

She went off on her own and came back
smiling. 'Sorted,' she said.

By the time Rachel's mum came home everything was clean and tidy.

'Come and sit down,' said Rachel. 'We've got a surprise for you.'

A few minutes later there was a knock at the back door. In walked Mrs. Clarke, Lu's mum. She handed Lu a big bag.

'Here we are,' said Rachel. 'It's Chinese tonight!'

Siti's Sisters
The early years

– one year on:
the Sisters
are older

– another year on:
The Sisters have
grown up (well,
nearly …)